This silly book
belongs to:

_____

To Lily,
my inspiration

BEACH LANE BOOKS • An imprint of Simon & Schuster Children's Publishing Division • 1230 Avenue of the Americas, New York, New York 10020 • Copyright © 2015 by Ken Krug • All rights reserved, including the right of reproduction in whole or in part in any form. • BEACH LANE BOOKS is a trademark of Simon & Schuster, Inc. • For information about special discounts for bulk purchases, please contact Simon & Schuster Special Sales at 1-866-506-1949 or business@simonandschuster.com. • The Simon & Schuster Speakers Bureau can bring authors to your live event. For more information or to book an event, contact the Simon & Schuster Speakers Bureau at 1-866-248-3049 or visit our website at www.simonspeakers.com. • Book design by Lauren Rille • The text for this book is set in Archer. • The illustrations for this book are rendered in oil paint on paper. • Manufactured in China • 1114 SCP • First Edition • 10 9 8 7 6 5 4 3 2 1 • Library of Congress Cataloging-in-Publication Data • Krug, Ken, author, illustrator. • No, silly! / Ken Krug.—First edition. • p. cm. • Summary: As their mamas and dads listen, preschoolers describe favorite things to do. • ISBN 978-1-4814-0066-4 (hardcover) • ISBN 978-1-4814-0067-1 (eBook) • [1. Parent and child—Fiction.] I. Title. • PZ7.K9412No 2015 • [E]—dc23 • 2013048776

# No, Silly!

by Ken Krug

BEACH LANE BOOKS

New York · London · Toronto · Sydney · New Delhi

I like to sleep in my bed.

I like to sleep in my dad's big chair.

I like to sleep on my mama's lap.

And I like to sleep on cookies.

No, silly!
You *eat* cookies.

I like to eat corn.

I like to eat apples.

I like to eat ice cream.

And I like to eat books.

# No, silly!

You *read* books.

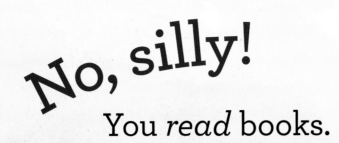

MUD PIE RECIPES

THE FOURTH LITTLE PIG

MICE 'I' NICE

I like to read letters.

I like to read cards.

I like to read signs.

And I like to read trucks.

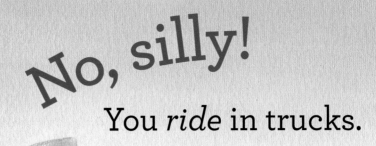

No, silly!

You *ride* in trucks.

I like to ride on my bike.

I like to ride on my dad.

I like to ride in airplanes.

And I like to ride in my bed.

No, silly!

You *sleep* in your bed.

But first I like to splash.

Then I like to snuggle.

Then I like to hug and kiss.

And then I like to put
Mama and Dad to bed.

Mama and Dad put *you* to bed.

Sweet dreams . . .